ANNA GROSSNICKLE HINES

WHEN
THE GOBLINS
CAME KNOCKING

 GREENWILLOW BOOKS, NEW YORK

The full-color art was prepared with colored
pencils on black paper.
The text type is Plantin.

Copyright © 1995 by Anna Grossnickle Hines
All rights reserved. No part of this book may
be reproduced or utilized in any form or by
any means, electronic or mechanical, including
photocopying, recording, or by any information
storage and retrieval system, without permission
in writing from the Publisher, Greenwillow Books,
a division of William Morrow & Company, Inc.,
1350 Avenue of the Americas, New York, NY 10019.
Printed in Hong Kong
by South China Printing Company (1988) Ltd.
First Edition
10 9 8 7 6 5 4 3 2 1

Library of Congress
Cataloging-in-Publication Data
Hines, Anna Grossnickle.
When the goblins came knocking /
by Anna Grossnickle Hines.
p.   cm.
Summary: Last Halloween was
a scary experience because of walking
pumpkins, haunting ghosts, flying
witches, and other disturbing sights,
but this Halloween will be different.
ISBN 0-688-13735-0 (trade).
ISBN 0-688-13736-9 (lib. bdg.)
[1. Halloween—Fiction.
2. Stories in rhyme.]
I. Title.   PZ8.3.H556Wh
1995   [E]—dc20
94-19366   CIP   AC

FOR JOCELYN AND ROY,
WHO HELP CHILDREN
AND THOSE WHO WORK WITH CHILDREN
UNDERSTAND THEIR FEELINGS

When the pumpkins came walking,
creeping and peeking,
sneakily stalking,
last Halloween . . .

I was tongue-tied.

When the ghosties came haunting,
moaning and groaning,
booing and taunting,
last Halloween . . .

I wanted to hide.

When the witches came flying,
screeching and cackling,
swooping and crying,
last Halloween . . .
I ran, terrified.

When the ghoulies came prancing,
smirking and grinning,
leaping and dancing,
last Halloween . . .
I trembled inside.

When the monsters came yowling,
screaming and shrieking,
yelling and howling,
last Halloween . . .
I whined and I cried.

When the goblins came knocking,
tricking and treating,
spooking and mocking,
last Halloween . . .
I was too scared to join in the fun.

But *this* Halloween . . . .

I'm the scariest one!